For Isla. S.D.
For Chris and Kai. C.C.

First American edition published in 2013 by Andersen Press USA,
an imprint of Andersen Press Ltd.
www.andersenpressusa.com

First published in Great Britain in 2013 by Andersen Press Ltd.,
20 Vauxhall Bridge Road, London SW1V 2SA.
Published in Australia by Random House Australia Pty.,
Level 3, 100 Pacific Highway, North Sydney, NSW 2060.

Distributed in the United States and Canada by
Lerner Publishing Group, Inc.
241 First Avenue North
Minneapolis, MN 55401 U.S.A.
www.lernerbooks.com

Color separated in Switzerland by Photolitho AG, Zürich.
Printed and bound in Malaysia by Tien Wah Press.
Christopher Corr has used gouache in this book.

Library Cataloging-in-Publication Data available.
ISBN: 978-1-4677-2028-1
eBook ISBN: 978-1-4677-2034-2

1 – TWP – 2/14/13
This book has been printed on acid-free paper

DON'T SPILL THE MILK!

Stephen Davies   Christopher Corr

ANDERSEN PRESS USA

Penda lived in a tiny village in Africa with her mum and her aunties. It was rainy season, so Penda's dad was up in the grasslands looking after the sheep.

"Penda," said her mum one day, "I'm going to take a bowl of
milk to Daddy. I will be back this afternoon."
"I know where the grasslands are," said Penda. "Let
me take Daddy his milk. Please, please, please!"

"All right," said her mum, "but try
not to spill any milk on the way."
Penda ran to milk the cow.
She filled a bowl, put it on her
head, stood up, and began to walk.

Steady, Penda whispered to herself. Gently does it, girl.
Don't wiggle, don't wobble, don't try to rush it, girl.

Penda picked a path across
the uppy, downy dunes,
past a caravan of camels and
a flock of desert jinns.

Don't slip, don't slide, girl, don't fall over.
Don't let a single droplet drop on the sand.

It was the day of the rainy-season mask dance.
Penda wove her way amid a million dancing beasties.

Walk tall, walk steady,
eyes on the horizon, girl.
Don't even think about
spilling any milk.

The great River Niger
was dark and wide.

Penda took a ride in
a stinky fishing boat.

Don't shiver, don't quiver,
don't fall in the river, girl.

Keep it on your head,
girl, milk don't float.

Fifteen pale giraffes were stalking across the plains
like fifteen aliens on a dusty moon.

Don't look, don't turn your head,
just walk on through. You're not at the zoo,
girl, you've got work to do.

Oh no! One final mountain looming high!
Penda breathed in deep, and up she climbed.

Left foot, right foot, never give up, girl.
Left hand, right hand, all the way up now.

At last Penda arrived
at the grasslands! A hundred sheep
were munching grass, and there
in the middle, chilling in the shade
of a mango tree, sat Penda's dad.

"Hi, Daddy."
"Hi, Penda. Nice to see you."
"I've brought you some milk," said Penda.
She took the bowl off her head, but just
as she was passing it to Daddy . . .

SPLOSH!

A big fat mango landed right in the bowl! Daddy's milk spilled everywhere.

"I don't believe it!" wailed Penda. "I carried that milk for miles and miles over the dunes and across the river and up the mountain, and I didn't stop to watch the mask dance or the white giraffes, because I didn't want to spill a single drop and now look — IT'S ALL GONE!"

Daddy gave Penda a big hug.
"It's not all gone," he whispered. "There was more than milk in that bowl."
"Huh?" said Penda.

"It's true," said Daddy. "Your love for me was in the bowl as well.
You carried it over the dunes and across the river and up the mountain.
You carried it past the mask dance and the white giraffes.
You brought it all the way up to the grasslands, and you gave it to me just fine.
This bowl was full of love, girl, and it still is. You didn't spill a drop."

Penda wiped away her tears.
She pointed at the big fat mango.
"I think it must be lunchtime,"
she said.

"I agree," said Daddy. "As it happens, I prefer mango to milk any day."
Daddy took a knife and cut the mango into three big, juicy pieces.

Penda ate the first piece.
"Yummy!" she said.
Daddy ate the second
piece. "Scrummy!" he said.

The third piece was still in
the bowl. "For Mummy?"
asked Penda.
"That's right," said Daddy.

"Tell her it comes with all my love!"

Author's Note

I have lived in Burkina Faso for more than ten years and regularly visit Mali and Niger. I wrote *Don't Spill the Milk!* specifically with Christopher Corr in mind. He is very good at portraying Africa's varied landscapes, so I chose a region that would show off this variety to the utmost. I chose the banks of the Niger River (in the West African country of the same name), and the Dosso Reserve, on the eastern bank of the Niger River, which I have visited on several occasions.

All the geographic features in the book are found in this area, as is the beautiful West African giraffe. The West African giraffe is paler than its East African counterpart and is an endangered species—only 310 remain.

Penda and her father are from the Fulani tribe. It is normal for Fulani herders to leave home in the rainy season and take their herds somewhere where they will not be able to get into fields and damage crops. The grasslands on the top of a hill in an unpopulated area would do nicely! Penda's brothers would no doubt have been left at home to cultivate the family's millet field, and so it is entirely feasible for a girl to undertake a journey in Niger that would take in dunes, the river, camels, and giraffes.

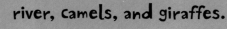